Katherine Applegate

Doggo AND Pupper

Illustrated by **Charlie Alder**

Feiwel and Friends

New York

For Ben, Luc, and—of course—Teddy.

—KA

For "Big Dog" Jonny A. and "Young Pup" Will A.

—CA

A Feiwel and Friends Book
An imprint of Macmillan Publishing Group, LLC
120 Broadway, New York, NY 10271
mackids.com

Library of Congress Cataloging-in-Publication Data is available.

First edition, 2021
Book design by Liz Dresner
Feiwel and Friends logo designed by Filomena Tuosto
The artist used a combination of collage and digital
techniques to create the illustrations for this book.
Printed in China by RR Donnelley Asia Printing Solutions Ltd.,
Dongguan City, Guangdong Province

ISBN 978-1-250-62097-2 (hardcover)
1 3 5 7 9 10 8 6 4 2

Contents

Chapter One

Same Old, Same Old

Every night Cat asked,
"How was your day,
Doggo?"

Every night Doggo said,
"Same old, same old."
   Then he would wink at the
smiling moon and say, "Could have
been worse."

3

Every day was just like every other day.
Doggo had many jobs.

Cook waker.

Nap taker.

4

Bug stalker.

Girl walker.

Crumb eater.

Mail greeter.

Trash diver.

Co-driver.

Book holder.

Squirrel scolder.

Bear finder.

Kid minder.

9

Treat smuggler.

Dream snuggler.

It was important to stay hydrated

and well-rested.

Bathroom

Even when the humans left, Doggo kept busy.

It was hard work.
But someone had to do it.

Chapter Two

The Idea

Sometimes Doggo missed the good old days.

But he was happy enough.
And happy enough was
fine with him.

The humans worried.

They said Doggo seemed bored.

They said his days were humdrum.

They said his life needed more zip and zing.

"You should shake things up," said Cat.

"I like my life just so," said Doggo.

"You used
to be fun,"
said Cat.

"I used to
be young,"
said Doggo.

"Watch out, Doggo," said Cat one day. "I think the humans have an idea."

She licked a paw. "Remember the last time they had an idea?"

Doggo remembered.

It was not pretty.

When the humans came home, Doggo hid.

It did not matter.
The idea found him, anyway.

Chapter Three

Pupper

Life with Pupper was not boring.

It was not
humdrum.

It was not the same old, same old.

Doggo tried to teach Pupper his jobs.

But Pupper was goofy.

Pupper was messy.

Pupper was having a ball.

Doggo tried to be
a good sport.

But Pupper was silly.

Pupper was lazy.

Pupper was having the time of his life.

Night was the worst.

Pupper did not
want to go to sleep.

He was full of zip and zing.

He wanted to hear stories.

He wanted to
ask questions.

Did someone chew the moon?
Can comets chase their tails?
Should I sing to the stars?

"The problem with Pupper is that he is a pest," said Doggo.

"The problem with Pupper is that he is a Pupper," said Cat.

"I was never like that," said Doggo. "Is that so," said Cat.

When the humans left, Pupper got
a bit carried away.

It was not pretty.

The humans were not happy.

"The problem with Pupper is that he has no manners," they said.

"We should send him to charm school."

"I want to stay here with you,"
Pupper told Doggo.
"I do not want to be charming."

"I went to charm school," said Doggo.
"And look at me."

Pupper hid.

It did not matter.

Chapter Four

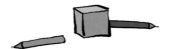

The New, Improved Pupper

Pupper learned to sit.

He learned to stay.

He learned to come.

After a while, he
stopped being goofy.

He stopped being messy.

He stopped having
a ball.

The humans were pleased.
"Pupper has manners," they said.

Doggo was pleased.

"Pupper is not a pest," he said.

Even when the
humans left, Pupper
kept busy with his
homework.

He did not bother Doggo at all.

Sometimes Doggo
forgot Pupper was
even there.

"Are you happy, Pupper?" Doggo asked.
"Happy enough," Pupper said.

"How was your day, Pupper?" Cat asked.
"Same old, same old," Pupper said.

Then he looked at the smiling moon and sighed.

Chapter Five

A New Idea

That night the moon was full.
Doggo could not sleep.
He wanted to tell stories.
He wanted to answer questions.

"Where are you going, Doggo?" Cat asked.
"I have an idea," he said.
She licked a paw. "Remember the last time you had an idea?"

Doggo remembered.
It was not pretty.

It took a while,
but Doggo found
what he needed.

When he woke the snoring humans,
they groaned.

"Sure," they said.
"Take the car. Good
luck getting very far."

"Pupper," Doggo whispered.
"Is it time to work?" Pupper asked.

"No," said Doggo.
"It is time to play.
"It is time to go
sing to the stars."

Chapter Six

Road Trip

It was a lovely night for a drive.

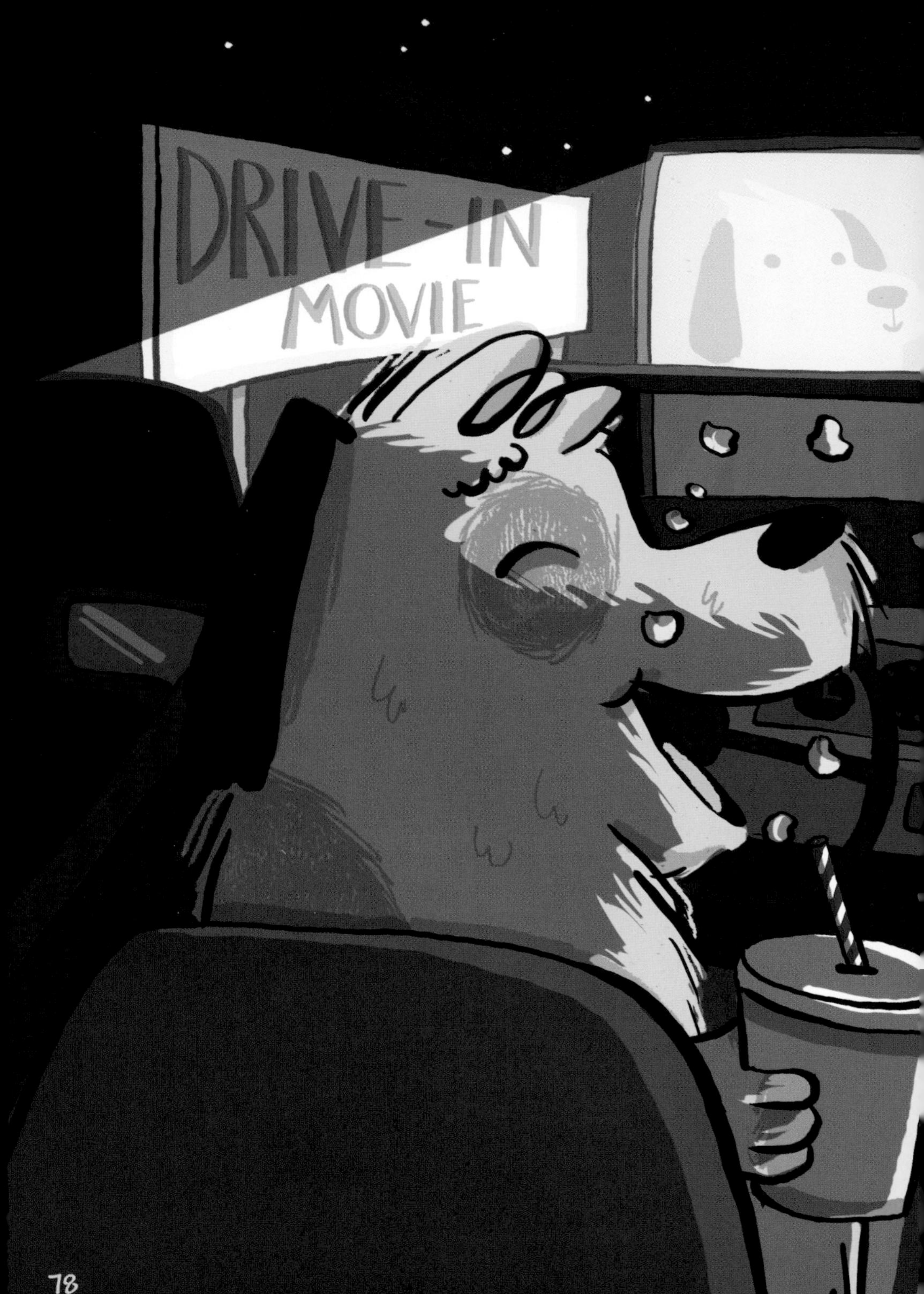
DRIVE-IN
MOVIE

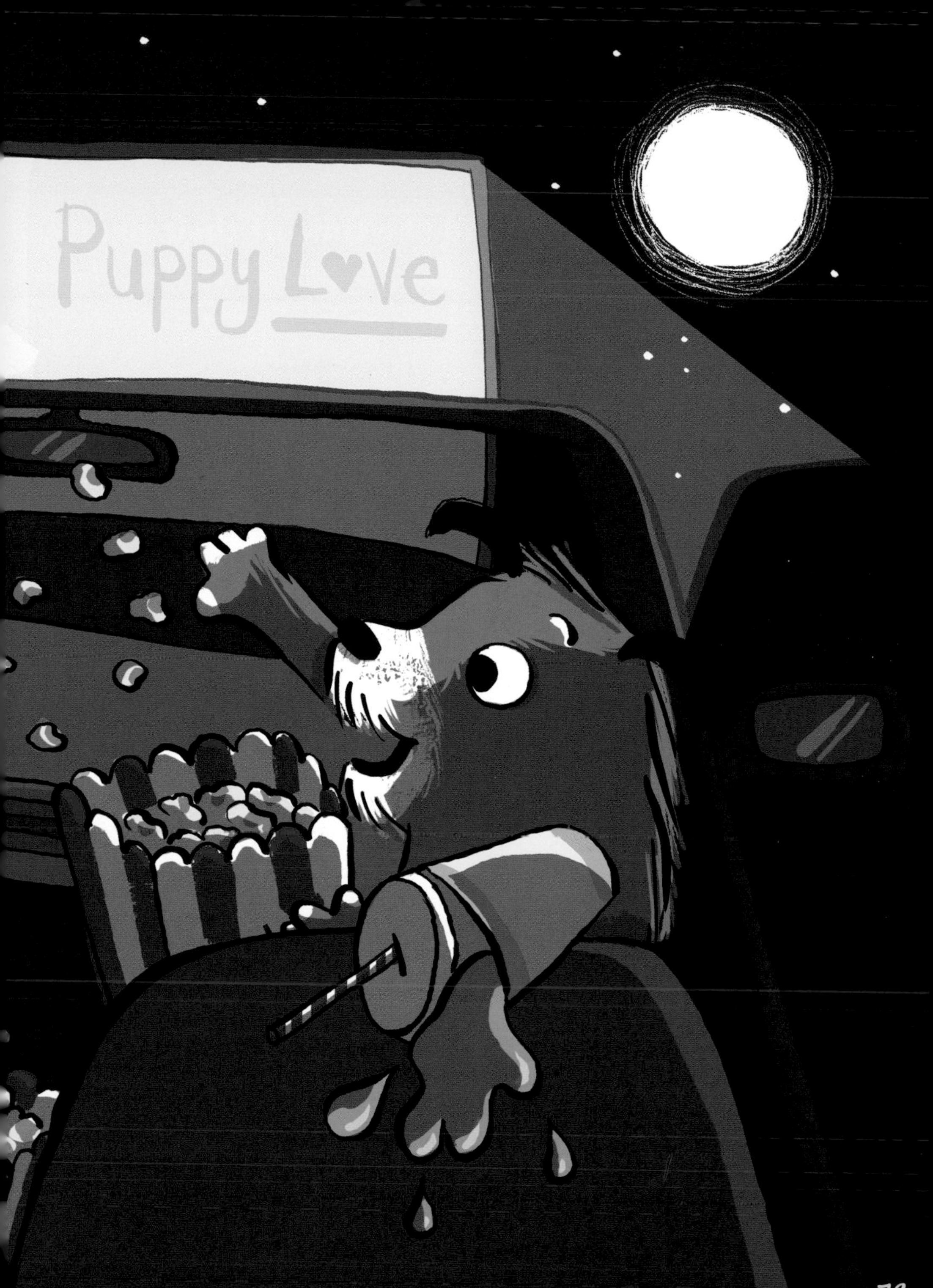
Puppy Love

Doggo and Pupper had the time of their lives.

Chapter
Seven

Home

The humans were still asleep when
Doggo and Pupper returned.

Doggo tucked Pupper into bed.

"How was your night, Doggo?" Cat asked.
"Could have been worse," said Doggo.
Cat licked a paw. "You don't say," she said.

The moon smiled.
And so did Doggo and Pupper.

Doggo's Guide to Puppies

Puppies are silly.

Puppies are curious.

Puppies like to chew.

Puppies like to make puddles . . . and other things.

Puppies need lots of naps.

Puppies need a special place to call their own.

Puppies need special food.

Puppies need rules.

Puppies need lots of play.

Puppies need lots of love.